Fools Rush In

Gail R. Delaney

Art
REQUIRES HEART
#SupportArtistsNotAI
www.GailDelaney.com

Fools Rush In Spotify Playlist

Do you like having a soundtrack to the books you read? I've created a playlist for "Fools Rush In" on Spotify.

You might see a trend. :-)

Chapter One

"Your father and Stacy will be at the house at six," Daniel Marsden's mother Vivian said through the phone, and he mentally applauded her for successfully silencing the usual derisive tone in her voice when she spoke of her ex-husband Charles Marsden. "Your sister and Horace will be here by half past. Horace had a late-day meeting scheduled last minute. I told them that was fine since you probably wouldn't be here until six yourself. Unless you think you can be here earlier..."

He sandwiched his phone between his ear and shoulder, trying to hold it while shifting a stack of marriage licenses and files he nearly managed to drop. "I doubt it, Ma. My night manager isn't here until six, and I don't want to short the staff in case there's an issue."

"What kind of issue could you possibly have, Danny? You run a wedding chapel, for goodness sake."

Daniel smiled and managed to get the stack in control and held it against his chest so he could take his phone in hand. "You'd be surprised at some of the stories I could tell you." He turned the corner of the hall leading past the preparation rooms and to the back office area. "And the later it gets, the crazier the stories. And it's Friday night. The only crazier night is Saturday."

"Perhaps you can provide us with some stories frightening enough to convince Rebecca and Horace they need to slow down and not rush into marriage."

"Ma, they've been dating for two years. How is that rushing?"

He reached his office, and as he curled his fingers around the doorknob, Jillian bolted around the corner behind him. He pushed open the door as he glanced over his shoulder, and the phone slid away from his ear at her wide-eyed panicked look.

"We have a runner," Jillian said in a stage whisper.

Daniel sighed and tried to hold up one finger, but nearly dropped his phone in the process. He bumped the office door with his hip, hoping to get inside and put down his papers before they scattered.

And stopped short when he saw a young woman, probably no older than him at thirty, dressed in a mid-calf cream silk dress, standing at the corner of his desk. Her cheeks were flushed and damp, her eyes red and wide. Rich brown hair framed her cheeks to fall around her mostly bare shoulders in a style reminiscent of a Golden Age Hollywood starlet. She even wore rich red lipstick and her eyes were lined to draw attention to thick lashes and upswept corners.

Their gazes met, and she shook her head, the tiniest of movements.

"Daniel, are you listening?"

Keeping his eyes on the woman, Daniel placed the papers on the couch by his door and stepped back out of the office, closing the door almost completely behind him, enough so the "runner" wouldn't be seen. He shifted his phone to his other hand so he could keep his left hand on the door.

"I'm sorry, Ma. One of those interesting stories seems to have come up. I'll be there as soon as I can after six, I promise."

Not waiting for her response, he tapped off the call, pocketed the phone, and turned to face Jillian. She bolted to him, standing close enough to whisper, glancing up and down the hall. "You haven't seen her, have you?"

"So, it's the bride this time?" he asked, hoping to sound convincing. As he kept his focus on Jillian, he pushed his hand into his pocket and pinched between his fingers the linen handkerchief he always carried.

"The couple who booked chapel four last week. Spalaris and Jackson."

Daniel nodded and shifted his weight to cover hooking his hand around the door. To Jillian, it would appear he leaned on the open door. Hopefully, Ms. Spalaris—whom he assumed was the woman hiding in his office—would see his hand. Moments later, with a small tug, the handkerchief left his fingers.

Jillian crossed her arms and huffed. "Though, I think she only beat the groom by minutes. I swear, he almost seemed relieved when I said I couldn't find her."

"You *told* him?" Daniel scolded. "Jillian—"

"I know, I know..." she said, shaking her head and holding up her hands in defense. "I didn't want to, but he pushed. But, I don't think she's *gone* gone. Her purse, luggage, and even her phone are still in the bride's ready room. I think she's just...hiding."

"Well, keep looking. If you need help, let me know. Otherwise..." He hooked his thumb over his shoulder toward his office door.

Jillian nodded, hands set at her slender waist. She huffed to blow some auburn hair off her forehead, then turned on her heels and headed back the way she came. Daniel slid his fingers into his front pockets, leaving his thumbs hanging out, and waited until she reached the hallway corner. She glanced back at him and offered a comical salute, and he smiled. As soon as she was out of sight, he let the smile go and turned back to his office door. They had at least one runner a week, but this had to be the first time he'd found said runner in his office. Usually, they ran right out the front door.

As long as he had the non-refundable ceremony deposit, he

figured it was for the best. If they felt the need to run out on their often quickie Vegas wedding, they weren't ready to get married.

Daniel curled his hand around the knob, took in a deep breath and puffed it out, then pushed open the door and stepped inside. His visitor had moved back to the corner of his desk, but had turned to face his window and spun around with a gasp when he came inside. He held her gaze as he eased the door closed again. Even then, she jumped when the latch clicked. As skittish as a newborn colt.

And beautiful. He'd noticed before but had been too shocked to let it register. She was beautiful. Not gorgeous. Not pretty. Not stunning. Beautiful. Gorgeous made you pause. Pretty made you smile. Beautiful bloomed in your chest. Odd, there was a distinct delineation in his head.

He pushed his hands into his pockets again, his thumbs hanging out, and took two steps toward her. "First time I've found a runaway bride in my office," he said, hoping his smile helped. He tried a few more steps toward her, and while she was still wide-eyed, she didn't move. Her skittishness concerned him; he tried to maintain his smile and fought the apprehension in his chest. "Miss, do you need help? Are you afraid of whoever it is waiting out there for you?"

His final step brought him close enough to her that he could touch her, but he wouldn't. Cardinal rule. Well, one of the cardinal rules. This close, he put her at probably five-four, since she had on good three-inch heels, and she was still at least four or five inches shorter than him. Her eyes were a rich chocolate brown, shining with tears as she stared up at him. Daniel pressed his lips together and released air through his nose.

"Miss, I need you to answer—"

She didn't say a word, but her face twisted in despair and she turned into his chest, her shoulders shaking. He had no choice but to embrace her, or they both would topple over. At a loss as to what else to do, he circled one arm across her shoulders, smoothed his other hand over her hair, and stood silent while her tears soaked his tee shirt.

"Water or champagne. Your choice."

Tessa looked up to the man standing in front of her, a glass of ice water in one hand, and a flute of chilled champagne in the other. Of course, a wedding chapel would have champagne on hand. She contemplated the water, but ultimately took the champagne, downing half of it before he sat down beside her.

"You might want to take it easy. Have you eaten anything?"

She shook her head, lowering the glass. The champagne was delicious, dry, crisp, and bubbly, but hit her empty stomach with a punch. "I don't think I can eat anything right now."

He stood again, the leather of the couch squeaking in protest, and crossed to his desk. He opened one of the side drawers, pulled out something, shut it again with a solid thunk, and then came back to the couch. Sitting again, he held out two small pouches of oyster crackers, the kind given out at restaurants or with takeout. "Try these."

Tessa shook her head, but he wrapped his fingers around her wrist and drew her arm toward him so her palm was up, and set the bags in her open hand.

"Trust me. You're going to want to eat."

Swallowing at the unexpected tingle where he'd briefly touched the inside of her wrist, she leaned forward enough to set the champagne flute on the floor by her feet and pulled open one of the bags. He watched and smiled when she conceded and put two of the little crackers in her mouth. The salt tasted good after the champagne, and she took two more.

"Thank you," she said, eating the food. At least she wasn't so screwed up as to forget decent manners. "For the crackers, the champagne." She lifted the now makeup-smeared handkerchief from where she'd rested it on her thigh. "The handkerchief. The office," she finished with an uncomfortable chuckle.

"Are you feeling better?" he asked, with his whiskey-smooth voice.

No man had the right to be so good-looking. It just wasn't fair. He was all rumpled, and casual, and...nope, just wasn't fair.

He had dark brown hair, kissed with enough sun to leave some lighter spots, so natural you knew he didn't do it on purpose, probably longer than his mother liked, because it waved and curled in a haphazard way that made her want to push it back from his forehead with her fingers. He wasn't the carefully styled, groomed, and body-conscious metrosexual type so prevalent in Los Angeles. Basic jeans, dark tee shirt—now with a wet spot in the middle of his chest from her breakdown—and brown loafers. He was likely Vegas, born and bred. Skin just tan enough to say he spent some time outside, but not much, since he worked here at the First, Last, Everything Wedding Chapel. Blue eyes, *of course*, and bone structure that was just...*wow*... with high cheekbones and a wide jawline.

But what hit her hardest was the genuine concern she acknowledged in his eyes. He watched her like he wanted to be sure she was okay, and hadn't implied once in the last ten minutes that she needed to leave.

The idea of leaving overrode her observations. Tessa downed the rest of the champagne. "I don't know. Is Eddie still looking for me?" she asked, choking down the last bit of bubbling courage.

He glanced toward his closed office door. "Probably," he said, grinning enough that deep dimples dug into his cheeks on each side of his mouth. "You didn't answer my question before," he said, his tone dropping into serious again. "Are you frightened of this...Eddie?"

Tessa closed her eyes and shook her head, already feeling the effects of the champagne. She shouldn't have drank it on an empty stomach, and so quickly. Her head felt funny like it floated an inch above her shoulders, and her movements were slightly out of sync. Tessa fished two more oyster crackers out of the first packet, finishing it off. She crumpled the cellophane to hold until she could throw it away, but the mystery man took it from her hand.

"The longer you take to answer, the more I'm convinced I need to have words with Mr. Jackson."

How did he know Eddie's name? Then her muddled brain worked out if he worked here, knowing made sense. With a sigh, she hunched forward to set her elbow on her knee and brace her forehead with her hand. "I'm sorry," she apologized. "I keep getting lost in my own head. I don't mean not to answer. No, I'm not frightened. Eddie is my best friend."

"Can I ask then why you're hiding in my office?"

She let her hand drop and looked at him. "Because he's my best friend. Not the *I'm-so-happy-to-be-married-to-my-best-friend* Hallmark card kind of best friend. He's my *played-in-the-treehouse-and-wore-our-underwear-to-run-under-the-hose-when-we-were-five* best friend."

He scowled, his lips turning down slightly, making his dimples disappear.

"Still not seeing the problem." He shook his head. With another long sigh, Tessa flopped back into the overstuffed cushions of the leather couch, hanging the hand holding the empty champagne glass over the arm. "One of the oldest clichés in the book. After a particularly rough breakup on both our parts, we promised each other if we were both single when we turned thirty—I turned thirty last week—we'd just marry each other and forget the whole 'someday my prince/princess will come' thing."

He groaned and shook his head, ending with an "Oh, man..."

"Seemed like a perfectly viable idea at the time. We like the same movies. We grew up in the same town. We know each other better than anyone else. Our parents are even friends. Who better to marry?"

"Except, what's there to find out?"

His insight surprised her; though, she supposed love and marriage were probably his specialty. You had to have some kind of insight into the human heart to run a wedding chapel, right? Kind of like running a bar.

Tessa extended her hand, waiting for him to take it, and did her level best to ignore the pleasant warmth of his skin once he did.

"Theresa Spalaris, recovering romantic and victim of pathetic clichés. But you can call me Tessa."

"Daniel Marsden, owner of a Vegas wedding chapel and vaguely disillusioned on the subject of love. Nice to meet you," he said, giving her hand a small squeeze rather than a shake.

"Nice to meet you," she said in return, letting go of his hand with a nudge of regret.

What was wrong with her? Was Daniel casting some kind of aphrodisiac mojo on her, or was she so terrified at the idea of marrying Eddie that she was looking for that instant zing her mother always told her about in a desperate attempt at avoiding her own decision?

He arched both eyebrows, one corner of his mouth tipping enough to reveal just one dimple. "Are you deep in thought, or do I have something stuck in my teeth?"

Tessa closed her eyes and shook her head, heat blooming in her cheeks. "Sorry. I'm just..." She opened her eyes again as she pushed her curled hair over her shoulder. "...distracted."

He took in a breath and opened his mouth as if he had something to say, but a knock at the door cut him short, and Tessa's pulse skyrocketed.

"Daniel, you got a second?" came a woman's voice, and she thought it might have been whoever had been talking to him in the hall earlier.

And looking for her.

He brought a finger to his lips, then whispered. "Are you ready to be found?"

She pulled a face, and he switched the single finger to an open palm and nodded once. "Hang on a second," he said for the benefit of whoever was in the hall.

He stood and offered his hand to draw her to her feet since the couch was visible as soon as the door opened. Daniel guided her to the other side of the door, where she'd be hidden, and with his hands at her waist, nudged her back until she was against the wall. Her pulse was still racing, but she was pretty sure it wasn't over whoever was outside. If he moved his hands, he could cover her stomach, his hands were so big.

Once again, he brought his finger to his lips, and she nodded her understanding. Then holding her gaze for as long as possible, he unlocked the door and pulled it open. Tessa closed her eyes, she couldn't help it, and held her breath.

Chapter Two

"Sorry," Daniel said, hoping his smile was convincing. He opened the door enough to stand easily in the doorway with his hand hooked around the wood above his head, leaning into it. He shoved his other hand in his front pocket. *Act casual.* "Figured I'd lock it with a bride on the loose."

Jillian looked more frazzled than half an hour before, her hair a bit wilder like she'd been pushing her fingers through it. "Guess you answered my question, then. We can't find her *anywhere*, Daniel. All I can think is she really did—and pardon the cliché Vegas catch-phrase—*leave the building.* This Eddie Jackson guy is gonna pace a furrow in our red shag carpet."

Daniel shrugged. "Maybe it's not meant to be."

She smirked and chuckled. "This coming from the guy who believes in destiny and fate and all that serendipity stuff? The heart knows what the heart knows."

A faint giggle came from behind the door, and Daniel cleared his throat to cover the sound. "Yeah, the heart knows..." he said, huffing a breath through his nose. "And maybe this runaway bride's heart knows this isn't right. Not everyone who pays the fee and says their vows are meant to be, ya know."

"Oy," Jillian said. "You're gonna start spouting poetry soon. I'm gonna go keep looking for Julia Roberts."

She headed back down the hall away from his office, mumbling to herself, and Daniel stood with the door open until she was out of sight, then eased the door shut again and turned the lock before looking at Tessa. She leaned back against the wall, with her hands tucked behind her, which angled her hips forward, an amused, closed-lip smirk on her brightly painted lips.

He returned the smile.

"So, you're the romantic type, huh?" she asked, arching an eyebrow. "I suppose I should have guessed. I mean, you *do* run a wedding chapel and all."

"It's worse than that," he admitted, turning toward her, and pushing his hands into his pockets. Seemed safer. Less likelihood they'd act on their own and do something foolish like touch her. "I *own* a wedding chapel."

Her dark eyes widened. "Just how does one go about deciding to own a wedding chapel in Vegas?"

"One graduates with an MBA in business management, and looks around his hometown to see what he can do with it." He shrugged. "I could run a casino, run a hotel, or run a wedding chapel. There aren't all that many industry variations in Vegas."

She hummed, that sexy smirk on her lips. Did she know how appealing her smile was? How appalled would she be if she knew the owner of the wedding chapel where she was supposed to be getting married found her appealing?

To put it lightly.

Despite his parents' rocky, broken love story, Daniel had always hung on to the idea of the happily ever after. Perhaps in protest of their story. This had to be the universe's cruel way of teaching him there was no such thing as serendipity or fate, because how much could fate suck if he met a woman who gut-punched him in the best possible way on her wedding day to someone else. Beyond the first tearful moments, Daniel found it easy and natural to talk with her, even joke with her, and he'd fought the instinctive urge to touch her from the moment she embraced him. He'd managed to indulge only once when he took her wrist to give her the crackers.

Then there was brushing his fingers on her skin to take back the wrapping when she was done.

Then he helped her up from the couch and held on to her hand a second longer than necessary, and then set his hands at her waist to guide her behind the door. He certainly could have just as easily said "Stand there", but silence had warranted the contact.

Hadn't it?

Okay, so one indulgence was an understatement.

"You're also a romantic?" She turned in his direction and leaned her shoulder into the wall beside the door, crossing her arms across her body, long, delicate fingers with nails painted a red to match her lipstick resting on her bare forearms.

Daniel tilted his head and looked past her. "Once, *just once,* I told Jillian I liked to think love and fate went hand in hand, and she's decided that makes me a romantic."

Tessa moved away from the wall and walked past him, her bare shoulder brushing his arm as she moved by, a subtle mix of sandalwood and floral scents rising to him, just enough to make him inhale to catch and appreciate the tingle in his nose.

"I'm a recovering romantic," she admitted, going to his desk where she leaned on the edge, her arms straight at her side and her hands curled around the front. The position emphasized the dip of her clavicles and the line of her exposed shoulders.

"Recovering..." he led, following so he stood close, but not too close.

She gave him a sideways look, an eyebrow arched. "I gave up so wholly on love I'm marrying my best friend. I believed love at first sight was possible." She shrugged. "I suppose I still do. Just maybe not for me. It's not for everyone."

"You have to be open to it," he said before he thought better of it.

She met his gaze, and he swore his heart jumped ahead a few beats, then lowered her lashes and looked down with a sigh. "I grew up with the idea of love at first sight. I'm a product of it," she said with a sentimental smile. "My parents met at a graduation party. They'd attended the same college for four years, but hadn't ever met until the night before they graduated. Both say it was instant and complete." Her expression was soft, like she loved the story, and her smile tipped up a little more. "They were married six weeks later." She looked at him again. "Still are married. Still insanely in love. So, see? Fate and love have a lot to live up to in my world."

"And yet, you're marrying someone you don't love." He didn't ask it as a question, since the answer seemed obvious.

Tessa stood from the edge of the desk. "Oh, no! I love Eddie. I do." She pressed her hand to her chest. "He has been there for me, beside me, through every good and bad thing in my life. He's wonderful." There was no hint of forced sincerity in her voice.

Daniel arched an eyebrow. "So why are you hiding in my office?"

She slumped into her previous position on the edge of the desk. "Because it's not a sizzle kind of love." It was a straightforward answer, and Daniel was pretty clear on what she meant, but she continued and he let her. "Mom always told me a love should sizzle. Wait for the sizzle." Her last words were softer, and she turned her face away from him toward the window.

Daniel cleared his throat and took a step closer to her. "Tessa, you've known me all of an hour and you can tell me to go to hell, but I have to wonder why you would settle for a marriage you don't want. Why settle?"

When she looked at him, her broken heart shadowing her eyes nearly demanded he reach for her, but he pushed his hands into his pockets.

"I promised," she said barely above a whisper. "I've never broken a promise I ever made to Eddie, and he's never broken a promise he made to me. He's my best friend. I can't..."

She turned away again, swallowing. "I just need some time."

"My people are in the middle of a situation right now," Daniel said into the phone call. Tessa dared a look in his direction; he grinned and winked. "I'll meet you in the vestibule in ten minutes."

She smiled and shook her head, trying not to eavesdrop any more than she could help, but it was tough with the two of them being the only ones in his office. So she stood by the window, looking out on a courtyard with a gazebo, hanging silk lanterns, and strings of lights. It was still afternoon, so nothing was lit, but she would bet the court-yard would be lovely after dark. And after it cooled down a bit. Los Angeles was hot in the summer, but Vegas was like the surface of the sun. Where she stood inches from the window, the heat radiated through the glass, a contrast to the cool air conditioning blowing on her back.

"Great. Thanks, George. See you in a few minutes."

Daniel hung up his phone and his desk chair wheels squeaked as he rolled across his wood floor. Tessa kept her back to him, finding it more difficult to hold her thoughts in line if she didn't. A terrible dread had settled into her chest as the hour passed, and she struggled with her thoughts. Her reactions.

She'd grown up hearing the story of how completely and quickly her parents had fallen in love. She'd asked her mother to tell her the story time and again, and when she was in her late teens but consid-ered old enough to date, her mother still told the story but with a different tone.

Wait for it, Theresa. I wish I'd known love could be like this. I wish someone had told me. I would have been content knowing the day would come when your father came into my life. And I wouldn't have questioned it.

"Sorry about that," Daniel said, stepping behind her so his voice hit close to her ear, and a massive butterfly did a somersault in her stomach.

"I should be apologizing to you," she said, tilting her head back enough to look at him over her shoulder, which required she look up. After she slipped off her high heels, he was several inches taller than her. "I'm the one disrupting your day." She smiled, but it felt forced. "I'm sorry."

"Don't be sorry," he said with the lopsided grin she already recognized and appreciated. "The best day I've had in a long time."

His blue eyes shifted, and his gaze along her hair, her face, down to her shoulder was as tactile as a touch and she had to fight hard against the shiver. She wanted to weep. This was the flash and the consumption her mother told her about, but why did she have to meet Daniel Marsden *today*? On her supposed wedding day?

Because how else would I have met him?

He widened his smile a degree. "You have a million thoughts swirling around in your head, don't you." He didn't ask it as a question. "Tell me some of them."

"Do you think love and fate walk hand in hand?" she asked, the ill-advised question out of her mouth before her conscience could remind her again she had no place asking such things.

He took a single step closer, close enough if she leaned back just a little bit she'd brush against him, but not so close they would touch if she didn't move. She wanted to move. Desperately. Instead, she crossed her arms and took in a slow breath. Daniel's focus was down, somewhere around her shoulder, and when he exhaled his breath warmed her skin. Did he have any idea what he did to her? Did he have any idea how close to making a fool of herself she truly was?

"I do," he finally said. "But I believe it only if you're open to it. I believe everyone is given that chance, but too many times they ignore it because they rationalize it away." He raised his, but his gaze settled on her mouth and her heart wanted to pound out of her chest. "My story is very different than yours." His lips tipped up at one corner and he chuckled. "Polar opposite actually." Finally, he looked her in the eyes and she could breathe again. "My parents dated and were engaged longer than they were married. They were together twelve years before they married, and they only married then because Mom realized she was pregnant with me. They had my sister a couple of years later, and divorced after nine years."

"I'm sorry..." she said automatically, but her heart meant it.

"Trust me, divorce was better than the fighting. They remain aggressively civil."

He shifted the weight on his feet and pushed his hands into his pockets in a way she'd also already learned to recognize, but the action made his arm brush her back. He didn't move, and neither did she. His skin was warm, and she was keenly away of every point of contact.

That butterfly took flight again.

"Thing is, I suspect my mother had one of those moments, one of those meetings. The kind that changes you. But she had been with my father for a few months, and she knew her parents would have considered him better husband material. She told me once she loved my father, but their passion came from fighting not from living." He watched her down the line of his nose, and she had to keep her head tipped back to see his face. "Does that make sense?"

Tessa nodded. "You do know you—the you that you are—wouldn't be alive if she had gone with this other man."

Daniel canted his head, shrugging his shoulder toward his tilted ear. "Maybe, but Mom might have been happy. And don't think I don't realize I'm partially the reason."

Tessa turned in the space between him and the window, reaching out before her head overrode her heart, and laid her hand on his chest. "Oh, Daniel. I can't imagine your mother would say that—"

"She never did," he said gently, then glanced at where she rested her hand and took a long, deep breath. "I just have to wonder what her world would have been like if she had grabbed hold of happiness when it stood..." He raised his head and looked at her. "...right in front of her."

Tessa curled her fingers, tugging at the soft fabric of his tee shirt, and tried to find a thought that could make it through the thumping of her heartbeat in her ears. The desk phone rang and she startled, gasping. Daniel laid his hand over hers and drew it from his chest, stepping away to answer the phone.

She blinked and swallowed against the scratch in her throat. Her eyes were wet, her throat dry, and her pulse so rapid she was dizzy. Only vaguely did she hear his side of the call, and then he hung up again.

"I have to go up front," he said.

She couldn't turn, couldn't think.

"Tessa," he said louder.

With a hard intake of air, she turned enough to see him and nodded; the extent of her abilities. He picked up a set of keys from the desk and headed for the door. "I'll lock it so no one will come in." He stopped at the door, his hand on the knob, and focused on her. "Unless you want me to leave it open."

"Lock it," she managed to rasp out. "Please."

With another nod, he left the office and seconds later the lock clicked into place. Tessa huffed in another deep breath, panting to steady her rushing pulse, and leaned on the windowsill. With hot tears in her eyes, she looked to the ceiling, silently begging for an answer.

Chapter Three

"We need different areas of the courtyard to represent different types of ceremonies and venues," Daniel explained, moving his extended arm from left to right to encompass the underdeveloped areas of the back property. "And each must be situated so that photographs taken in one wouldn't pick up parts of another. Secluded, but open. We still have a lot of walk in traffic, but we have more people planning ahead and wanting to reserve for certain types of ceremonies."

"How many people should each area be able to accommodate?" George asked, taking notes on a yellow notepad.

"One-fifty comfortably, two hundred if they don't mind getting close. That's really the max we want to try to fit. With the full overhaul of the banquet hall and kitchen, we'll be able to host receptions, too, but I intend for this to remain a smaller venue even for those who plan ahead. We can host two receptions at a time if we remodel right."

"When do you want this done?" George asked, looking up from his notes.

Daniel sighed, pushing his hands into his pockets. "We've missed the summer rush, but I'd like to see it done by early October to get the fall jump." He looked to his long-time contractor. "That doable?"

George grinned, showing off a gap in his grin where an incisor should be. "Sure, Mr. Marsden. You want it, you get it."

Not always.

"I'm finalizing the plans with the architectural firm at the end of this week. I'll send them when we're done so you can finish the quote."

George nodded and closed his notebook, shoving it into the ragged briefcase he carried, a corner with furled pages sticking up when it didn't go in straight. "We're on it."

Daniel stood in the shade cast by the slatted veranda cover, looking out over the courtyard. It was workable and had hosted plenty of weddings, but it was time to step up the game. He'd been excited about the plans, and even about George coming to finish the quote, but today he was distracted.

Unbidden, he turned his head enough to glance toward his office window on the other side of the courtyard. A glimpse of cream silk was enough to make him take in a deeper breath. She stood at the edge of the window, and perhaps anyone not expecting to see a beautiful woman in his office, wouldn't even notice.

But he noticed. He couldn't *not* notice.

"Everything good, Mr. Marsden?" George asked, pulling Daniel back from his thoughts. "You seem out of it today if you don't mind me saying so."

Daniel shook his head, looking back to the contractor. "I don't mind, George. It's an accurate description." With a sharp intake of air, he pivoted and motioned with a tilt of his head for George to follow. "I'll walk you out."

Stepping into the interior of the chapel was instantly refreshing. It would hit 115 today by 3:00, and they always kept the inside much cooler than probably necessary to help with nerves. But air conditioning wasn't enough for some cases. He walked George back to the front, the sound of a processional march coming from the only currently occupied sanctuary. Tessa's wedding was one of four they had scheduled today; he'd checked when he left her alone. She and Eddie had called ahead two weeks to reserve the vintage chapel, which explained her Hollywood starlet look.

What would she look like without the dramatic makeup? He had no doubt she'd be just as beautiful.

Neither had brought anyone with them...family, friends, or otherwise. They'd requested witnesses be provided, and no reception following. If he didn't know better, he'd suspect neither of them had their heart in any part of the process. Tessa's certainly wasn't.

"I'll send along the plans in a few days," he reiterated to George, shook the man's large, calloused, deeply tanned hand, and stood at the welcome desk until George slipped on his sunglasses and went out the front door.

Maddie, their front desk receptionist and backup notary public, smiled at him as he turned. Her smile slipped and her brow pulled down. "Mr. Marsden, you feel okay?"

Daniel chuckled. "Apparently not." He pointed in the general direction of the hall and his office. "I'll be in my office."

She nodded. "Sure. Jillian was looking for you. I said you were with the contractor. The runaway bride is still on the run, and she is wondering if we should call the police."

"No," Daniel said, probably too quickly. "No. I'm sure she'll come out of hiding when she's ready."

Maddie smiled and went back to her computer. While walking down the hall, he passed by one of the empty chapels and a male voice caught his attention. Since other than the completing wedding, there should only be a couple of other people in the building, his gut instinct said it was probably Tessa's Eddie.

Just the concept of *Tessa's Eddie* made his face contort.

Knowing it was low down and no good of him, Daniel stopped outside the door. Yes, this was downright awful.

"Mom, I can't leave. Not until I know she's okay." He paused, and

Daniel held his breath, inching forward to risk a glance around the doorframe.

Geez, Eddie would give Idris Elba and Shemar Moore a run for Best Looking Bachelor, right down to the broad shoulders and movie-star-worthy chiseled jawline. Daniel wasn't usually one to check out other men, but this wasn't anyone, this was competition.

Wait, what?

"She's probably just scared. God knows I am." Another pause, then a sigh. "Who better to marry than my best friend? I'd be considered a very lucky man to have her as my wife. You've said as much how many times?"

Daniel's conscience finally won and with a clench of his jaw, he stomped past the open doorway. Eddie looked up, phone still to his ear, as Daniel passed but he didn't acknowledge the man. He couldn't meet the eyes of the guy who he'd do anything to steal his girl from him.

He rounded the corner and nearly collided with Jillian, pulling up short to keep from knocking them both on their backsides. Jillian gasped and grabbed his arm.

"Geez, Daniel, you're almost as hard to track down as our missing bride." She huffed, not giving him a chance to respond. "Did Maddie tell you I was looking for you? I think maybe we should call the police. I mean, what if something happened to this woman?"

Daniel shook his head as soon as she started with "*I think...*" cutting her off from any further argument as soon as she finished her question. "No. I guarantee the moment the cops show up, so would she, and then we've got a false report over our heads."

"It's not like *we* filed a false report," she said, her voice pitching up.

He brought his finger to his lip, shushing her. "The potential groom is around the corner," he said in a whisper, pointing back the way he came.

Jillian hissed air through her teeth, pulling her lips back as she looked past Daniel. "Okay, sorry. But how long do we wait?"

"Give it another half hour," he said and hated even saying it. One way or another, he'd have to convince a woman he didn't *want* to leave that she should. He had to work his jaw and force himself to speak. "I'm positive she'll show up by then."

It took Tessa almost ten minutes to convince herself to sit at Daniel's desk, and another five to pick up the phone, and by then she was afraid he would come back while she was on the call, and she hung up again. She didn't have the impression he would be bothered or upset if she used his phone, but she didn't know if she could have this conversation with him in the room.

But since she had left her phone in the bride's room, along with everything else, her choices were limited to using his phone...or daring to leave the office. Leave, be seen, and her hand would be forced.

She huffed and picked up the phone again, dialing in the familiar number. It only took two rings for her mother to pick up. "Hello?" her mother said, clearly and likely confused by the caller ID.

"Mom," Tessa tried to say, but her voice cracked and she had to clear her throat. "Mom, it's me."

"Theresa? Honey, what's wrong? Diana called here a bit ago wanting to know if I'd heard from you."

Tessa closed her eyes and supported her head with her hand across her brow. Of course, Diana had called her mother, they were best friends after all. Same as their children.

"You don't want to do this, do you, sweetheart."

Her mother's non-question twisted a sob out of Tessa's chest, and she tried hard to muffle it, but couldn't. She sucked in hard, afraid her ribs would collapse in on themselves, and gripped the phone like a lifeline.

"Oh, sweetheart," her mom whispered. "I was so afraid this would happen. I know you love Eddie, and I know you made him a promise, but he isn't where your heart lies. You haven't found that place yet."

Tessa sniffed in a deep breath and huffed it out, raising her head from her hands. On the corner of Daniel's desk beside his phone was a photograph of him with a group of people, and if she had to guess, she'd say his family. Beside him was a woman who appeared a bit younger, but her longer hair had the same rebellious wave his did, even though he wore his shorter, and they had the same smile. Beside Daniel stood a man his height, with the telltale wave in mostly gray hair, more salt than pepper. He had one hand on Daniel's shoulder, the other on Daniel's arm, and smiled at the camera. Beside the woman—Daniel's sister—was a woman several inches shorter than both Daniel and his sister. Her attention wasn't on the camera, but on her children, and her smile was present but not honest. She looked not unhappy, but not happy either. Would that be Tessa in a few years? Present, but distant? Would she have children, and would they know she was unhappy with her life?

"Theresa?" her mother urged.

"Mama," she said just above a whisper, falling back into the name she'd called her mother when she was young. "How did it feel the first time you saw Daddy? Not the first time you talked to him, or anything, but the first time you saw him?"

Her mother's light sigh carried through the phone, and in it, Tessa heard the smile. "I caught a glimpse of him a few feet away as I looked around the party for my friends, and I immediately had to turn back again. There was something about him that gripped me, held my attention as sure as if he'd waved a sign that said *Here I am, Aubrey. You've been looking for me*. Then he stared right at me, and—"

"You knew," Tessa finished.

"Sweetheart..." The tone in her mother's voice said more than her words that she had already figured out her daughter's dilemma. "Do you know?"

Tessa sniffed and wiped her cheeks. "I think so, Mama. But what if it's just me seeking a way out of this? What if—"

"Even if that were true, wouldn't it mean you don't want to marry Eddie? Theresa, I adore Eddie. You know that. I know you care for him. But you deserve a love that makes you feel alive, not makes you cry. You deserve it, and so does he."

"Not everyone finds love like you and Daddy," she said, not quite believing her own argument.

"Love is there for everyone. Don't rationalize it away for the sake of a promise I don't believe either one of you wants to keep."

"I believe it only if you're open to it. I believe everyone is given that chance, but too many times they ignore it because they rationalize it away."

Daniel had said practically the same thing. Gooseflesh rose on her arms and up her neck.

"What if instead of rationalizing away the maybe love I think I might have found, I'm using something fleeting and not real to rationalize away a love I found a long time ago and was too young to see it? What if Eddie *is* that lifetime love, but I don't recognize it anymore because we've known each other so long? What if I have a chance at the best kind of marriage, but I toss it away for a guy with great bone structure and beautiful eyes because I think finding him attractive equals falling in love?"

Her mother sighed, the sound heavy and wistful. "That's something you need to figure out, sweetheart. And you need to figure it out soon. For everyone's sake."

Chapter Four

Tessa stared into the mirror of Daniel's attached bathroom, disgusted at the destruction her crying jags had done to her carefully applied vintage makeup job. She looked more like a raccoon than a woman, let alone a bride or starlet. One look at her, and Eddie might call it off anyway.

She chuckled and ran her fingers through her hair. The dry Vegas air made it crackle with static and the curl had begun to relax. On the counter was a bit of a broken shoelace someone hadn't tossed in the trash yet, and after quickly plaiting her hair on the side so it hung in front of her left shoulder, she tied the broken lace to the bottom. If and when she decided to go through with the ceremony, she'd ask Eddie for a few minutes to touch up her makeup, but her hair was likely a lost cause.

Take her as she was, or don't take her at all. Not like he hadn't seen her at her worst already.

Not wanting to rummage around too much, Tessa staunchly avoided the medicine cabinet and opened the drawers of the vanity, finding some folded washcloths in the second. Warm water would have to do, and after a few minutes, her skin was rosy from scrubbing and her dramatic makeup was gone. Better to start with a clean slate. She looked again in the mirror and sighed. Plain Tessa again. She was quite the picture in her silk dress, braided hair, and makeup free face. Like a little girl playing dress up.

Stepping out into the office again, she immediately crossed her arms at the cold burst of air coming from the ceiling vents. In comparison to the bathroom, the office was much colder. A hooded sweatshirt in dark blue draped the arm of the couch furthest from the door, the opposite end from where she had sat an hour or so before, and she picked it up. A red "B" emblazoned the left chest, and "Red Sox Nation" was embroidered across the shoulders.

Tessa smiled. Maybe they were meant to be after all. Anyone who loved the BoSox was certainly worth consideration.

The lock disengaged and the door opened just as she wrapped herself in the oversized sweatshirt. She had to push the sleeves up her arm or they hung three inches past her fingertips. Daniel glanced around as he stepped in, then spotted her, and stopped stock still, his mouth open and his eyes slightly wide.

Heat hit her cheeks, and Tessa crossed her arms with a shrug beneath the big hoodie. "This is me," she said by way of apology. "Minus the professional makeup and hair. I hope you don't mind—" She unfolded her arms to hook a thumb over her shoulder toward the bathroom door behind her.

"No," he croaked and finished coming into the office, shutting the door behind him, never looking away from her. "I-I'm sorry that took so long. We're planning some renovations." He cleared his throat and shook his head just enough to count as a motion. "Tessa, you're beautiful."

She laughed and walked by him to the window. She liked that spot and felt she could hide enough behind the curtain she wouldn't be seen. Who would be looking for her here anyway? At the window, she glanced back at him; he stood in the same spot, still watching her.

"I bet you say that to all the runaway brides who sneak into your office to hide from their pending nuptials."

One corner of his mouth quirked. "Well, you're the first this... ever." Then he seemed to focus again, cleared his throat, and walked to her with his hands in his pockets. "I'm sorry it's cold in here. We have to keep it cooler to combat the desert heat, to make sure our clients are comfortable." He winced.

"What?" she asked. "Why did you wince?"

"I guess standing here beside you makes me dislike the word client." When he focused on her, he canted his head just slightly, his eyes shifting down to focus on her mouth. "If you're a client, it means you're here to marry someone else."

Her heart pounded so hard and so fast, she had to slip her hand beneath the fleece hoodie to press her palm over her breast. Her throat wanted to deprive her of oxygen and her head felt oddly heavy and light at the same time. Trying to keep her composure, Tessa raised her chin to look up at him and he met her gaze. "Daniel, do you have any idea how hard it is for me to think about—how *easy* it is for me to forget—why I'm here when you look at me like that? When you say things like that?"

He swallowed hard and drew his lips closer together, the simple shift of expression enhancing the lines of his cheekbones and jaw, and she had to clench her fists hidden within the hoodie to keep herself from reaching up to touch his cheek.

"Yeah, I'm pretty sure I do, because it takes about three seconds through that office door for me to forget you're here to marry someone else and not here for...me." The last word was little more than a breath.

His lean into her was by degrees only, the tilting of his head minuscule, but it was enough to make Tessa's breath catch and her body willfully toed-up just a tiny bit, drawn to the magnet in his chest that seemed to pull her. Just as quickly, but with far more strength of will, she stumbled a step back and turned away, creating space between them so she could breathe.

"I'm sorry," Daniel said behind her, his voice so earnest it made her heart ache. All she could manage was a shake of her head. "I don't intend to make this harder for you," he added, then sighed, even that sound enough to make her throat ache. "You need to go soon. My staff is pushing to call the police—"

She spun to face him, gasping.

"—if they don't find you in the next half hour or so," he finished, his entire expression tainted with regret. "Were it any other day, any other situation, I probably would have had them call already," he said with a curl forward of his shoulders, his hands in his pockets again, an abstract kind of shrug. "I can't hold them off much longer than that, but both they and Eddie are worried something unimaginable has happened to you since you left everything behind."

Tessa pressed her lips together until the muscles of her face ached, willing away the lump in her throat and the burn in her eyes. She took two steps backward until she reached his desk, leaning with her hands curled around the edge. With her eyes closed, she sensed his movement toward her, the soft stir of air, and the unmistakable awareness his approach pushed against her body. She both silently begged him to reach for her, touch her, and begged him not to because it would be her undoing.

When he was beside her, she opened her eyes, looking down at where her hand rested...and his fingertips touched the wood just an inch from hers. His fingers were long, like a musician's, his nails blunt but clean and filed.

Everything was spiraling out of control, and soon she'd be forced to take the wheel and steer her ship in one direction or another. But right now, at this moment, she wanted something—anything—else to think about.

"Do you play an instrument?" she asked, raising her head. He already watched her, and she felt for a moment like a work of art being appreciated by a museum visitor.

His lips curled in a slow smile that exposed just a bit of his teeth. "Yeah," he said with a small chuckle. "Piano."

Tessa smiled. "I love piano. I play, too. You're a Red Sox fan?"

He nodded. "I live in Vegas, but I used to visit my father's brother in Boston every summer as a kid and he'd take me to Foxboro to watch them play."

"It's not easy being a Sox fan out here." She shook her head and settled on the desk edge. "I get teased incessantly for it at work."

"What do you do?"

Tessa sighed, adding a groan because she hated admitting what she did. "I'm an executive assistant to a talent scout in Los Angeles." She winked at him. "And my boss would just love you."

"Why do you say it that way?"

"Say *what* what way? That my boss would love you?"

He shook his head, tipping his chin toward her. "No, why do you say what you do like you do."

She rolled her eyes and turned on her valley accent. "Because it's so...LA. Everyone is in the industry, or knows someone in the industry, or wants to be in the industry."

"And you don't," he stated, not asking a question.

Tessa shook her head. "Not really, no, but it was an opportunity that presented itself and a girl's gotta work. What's your favorite color?" she asked, following her tangent.

"Now, hang on." An unheard chuckle laced his tone. "I want to know what you'd do if you could."

She shook her head. "My answer isn't politically correct enough. Feminist enough. Whatever."

"So? It's your answer. I want to hear it."

She contemplated for half a second making up something, just so she wouldn't give the honest answer. He canted his head, one eyebrow tilting up in silent question. Tessa huffed and crossed her arms, feeling a bit lost in the big sweatshirt. She looked away, but he leaned to stay within her peripheral vision, and she turned her attention back to him. "I want to be the best dang soccer mom that ever was," she said, trying to say it strong even though heat flushed her cheeks.

His expression softened and that tempting mouth of his tugged up first in one corner, then the other. "You didn't want to tell me you want to be a mom? What's wrong with that?"

"Because it's the 21st century and women have fought long and hard for the right to do what they want and—"

"And you want to be a mom," he said softer than her.

She inhaled and forced herself to relax, not seeing any condemnation in his expression. Eddie knew what she wanted, and had promised her she could have it without argument from him, but whenever she tried to picture their children she saw nothing. Tessa angled her head opposite his. With the closing of just a few inches... She had to blink and focus to keep from thinking bad, bad thoughts. "So, what's your favorite color?"

Daniel's smile was contagious, but warming her from the inside out at the same time. He curled his knuckles into the desk and leaned his thigh against the edge, bringing him a fraction closer without touching her. "Red."

"Really? Most every man I've ever known says blue."

He shook his head. "Nope. Red." The way he said it sounded more like a seduction than a statement of fact. "You'd look amazing in red."

"What's your favorite food?" she asked, trying desperately to steady her breathing. She'd given up on her racing heart.

"I don't have one."

She arched her eyebrows in surprise, and he chuckled.

"What I mean is I love food in general. I'll eat just about anything at any time." He patted his stomach with his free hand. "Mom tells me it'll catch up with me someday."

She looked down at his lean form, and so many dangerous thoughts battled to be free, but she somehow managed to keep them in line. "I love anything with peanut butter."

"I make an awesome Thai peanut chicken with this fresh ground peanut butter I buy at a natural foods market in Henderson. I'll make it for you..."

His voice trailed off at the same moment the realization of his simple offer hit them both. Tessa raised her chin and looked him in the eyes, such blue eyes. They weren't any kind of special blue—not like she read in romance novels, the color of a sea during a storm or anything like that—but they were a perfect blue for him. A perfect blue to her.

"If you met me yesterday, just standing in line at that grocery store, what would you have done?" she asked, barely able to project her voice enough for him to hear.

Daniel shifted his studying gaze over her face, and she swore she could feel a whisper touch wherever he looked. Her cheeks, her forehead, her lips. She held her breath, waiting for his answer, watching it form behind his blue, blue eyes. He parted his lips but didn't speak yet, and she wanted to grab his shirt and shake him until he did.

"I would have probably been unable to say anything right away," he finally said, looking her in the eyes, that smooth smile forming dimples on his cheeks. "I'd have been too struck by how beautiful you are, but if I were lucky enough to find myself in line behind you, I probably would have tried to make a joke or strike up some lame conversation just to hear your voice. And then..." The smile grew, whimsical and warm. "I would have introduced myself somehow, and I would have walked you out, and tried to get up enough nerve to ask if I could see you again."

"Why would you have to work up the nerve?"

"Because it's hard to talk when your heart is pounding and your palms are sweating and you are almost positive you just walked into your future."

Her eyes burned and she had to blink to keep him in focus. He raised his hand and ran his thumb across her cheek, watching the path his touch took, and she closed her eyes, giving in to the momentary indulgence of turning into his touch.

"And as soon as possible, without scaring you as much as you terrify me, I would have kissed you," he said softly. She opened her eyes again, and he was closer, just close enough to make her dizzy.

"And I would have kissed you again because I am positive, without any question, once I kissed you I wouldn't be able to stop."

"Daniel..." she whispered.

He pressed his lips together and lowered his hand, taking a step backward. "But that was yesterday and it didn't happen." He sucked in a deep breath and pushed his hands into his pockets. Did he do that all the time, or if it was a coping mechanism to keep from touching her as much as she wished he would?

And didn't at the same time.

"I heard Eddie talking to his mother on the phone on my way back here," he admitted, pausing to clench his jaw. "He's worried. He seems to care."

Tessa nodded, and on shaking legs moved away from the desk, shrugging off his borrowed sweatshirt as she did.

It was time.

She couldn't run anymore. She couldn't hide anymore. She was a big girl and she'd made choices, and made promises, and it was time to deal with her reality.

Standing at the end of the couch by the door, she pulled the broken shoelace from the end of her braid and ran her fingers through the plait to free it. Not the carefully styled curls she'd arrived with, but probably not terrifying. With her back to Daniel, she looked at him over her shoulder. "I'll go tell them I'm alive and nothing happened to me."

Except something has. Something life-changing has happened. To me.

Daniel pressed his lips together and nodded, his shoulders hunched with his arms straight, hands in those damn pockets. Using the wall as support, she slipped her feet into the high-heeled shoes she'd discarded, then smoothed a hand over her dress and sighed. She did well until she curled her hand around the doorknob, and then she felt sure her heart broke. It cracked down the middle.

Eddie was her best friend, and he wanted her to be happy. She knew that. But never once had he made her feel so alive as a few words from Daniel Marsden had accomplished. Daniel convinced her, without saying the words, that she was the sole focus of his attention. She was who he wanted to be with. Could she go her whole life never feeling like this again?

Daniel took a step toward her, and she sucked in a sharp breath and stumbled into his arms. He held her tighter than that first embrace when he hadn't known her name and only knew she was some hysterical woman in his office. He held her as if he wanted to hold her, his hands pressed to her back, his arms holding her so close he nearly lifted her off the floor. Tessa inhaled, taking in the smell of him—subtle but masculine, clean, and fresh—and nuzzled her face into the solid side of his neck. The slight rough of afternoon whiskers abraded her cheek, but she didn't care. Sucking in hard, she kissed his cheek, his jaw, then pushed herself away before she kissed his lips the way she wanted. Not able to look at him again, she yanked open the door and ran from the office.

Chapter Five

"We're so happy to see you're okay, Miss Spalaris," the woman Tessa had picked up was named Jillian said as she came back into the bride's room with a glass of ice water. "Is there anything else I can get you? I'm sure we could find something good to eat if you're hungry."

The idea of food made her stomach turn, and Tessa shook her head. Right now, she would have really preferred the cold champagne Daniel had given her two hours before. Had it really only been two hours? It felt like a lifetime ago. How could she ache for a loss when she barely had anything to miss? "No, thank you. This is fine."

Jillian stood half way between her and the door, hands linked in front of her. Was it a subconscious attempt at blocking her escape? "Your fiancé was very worried, as were we all. But honestly, I think he's as nervous as you are. You shouldn't be concerned, I mean I'm sure—"

"Have you let him know the prodigal bride has returned?" she asked, barely able to force the words from her throat. She took a long drink, unable to look the woman in the eyes. Guilt was a common bedfellow today; she had caused this poor woman a great deal of nervous moments in the last two hours.

"I was about to," Jillian said, and paused long enough for Tessa to feel her questioning gaze, forcing her to look up. "Is there anything in particular you'd like me to tell him?"

There it was. There was her out. Her redemption.

Tell him I went home. Tell him I am so sorry. Tell him I do love him, but...

She blinked hard and ran her fingers up and down the wet sides of the glass, condensation forming despite the cool air. "Could you please ask him to meet me in the chapel in ten minutes?" she finally managed, and added a smile for good measure, hoping it was convincing. "I need to freshen up. Make myself presentable."

"You're beautiful, Tessa." Damn Daniel's voice in her head!

Jillian beamed, likely convinced the day was not a lost cause. With a nod, she turned on her spunky heels and left the room, leaving Tessa alone with her thoughts. And her decisions. With a heavy heart, she went to the small suitcase she'd brought with a couple of changes of clothing, more comfortable shoes, and her own makeup. The façade of a vintage Hollywood starlet was long gone. If she was going to do this, she was going to do it as herself, and no one else. No painted face. No sky-high heels. She toed out of the shoes and slid the thin straps of the dress off her shoulders.

When she unzipped the case and flopped it open, goosebumps flashed up her arms and made her scalp tingle. She'd forgotten she'd packed this particular dress since her mind hadn't been on what would impress her new husband. It seemed odd to consider what Eddie would find appealing. It was one of her favorites, so an instant grab.

It couldn't be more perfect.

Daniel paced the length of his office, hands braced at his waist to keep from grabbing anything within arm's reach and chucking it against the wall. With his emotionally distorted view, and rising level of raging frustration, he was just as likely to throw whatever it was through the window instead.

His phone rang, his mother's ringtone, and he couldn't bring himself to pick it up. He loved his mother, but if he had to hear right now about how he needed to talk his sister out of rushing into a marriage after two years, he'd likely say things he probably—no, he *knew*—he'd regret. When his office line rang at the same time, he looked at it as the one moment of serendipity he could easily embrace that day and reached across the desk to snatch up the handset.

"Hello, Daniel Marsden," he snapped, realizing too late he sounded like an angry bear. His cell phone still trilled, and he picked it up to silence it and send the call to voicemail.

Sorry, Mom.

"Oh, um, I wasn't sure who would pick up. I just hit redial," said an unfamiliar woman's voice on the other end of the line.

"You've reached First, Last, Everything wedding chapel," he said, pinching the bridge of his nose. "Were you trying to reach someone else?" He focused hard to push down the frustration in his chest so whoever this wasn't didn't suffer the brunt of a bad day she had nothing to do with.

No, it wasn't a bad day. It was a beautiful day. Just a bad end.

"No, this is where I needed it. My daughter called me from this number maybe forty-five minutes ago. Theresa Spalaris."

"You're Tessa's mom..." Daniel said, realizing a second too late he shouldn't have been so formal. This woman had no idea who she was speaking to, or anything that had happened that day. He cleared his throat. "This is Daniel Marsden, I own the chapel. Your daughter was using my office earlier. I suppose she used my direct line to call you."

"Oh," she said, and if he didn't know better he heard the lilt of a smile in her tone. The more he listened, the more he heard the similarity between Tessa's voice and her mother's. A similar richness and familiarity scraped over his exposed nerves. "She was upset. I've been trying to reach her on her cell phone, but she hasn't been answering. Is she okay?"

"She's..." His voice cracked and he cleared his throat. "Excuse me, Mrs. Spalaris. She's fine."

"Is she with Eddie?"

The question was as effective as a punch in the chest by Evander Holyfield. Daniel leaned forward, bracing himself on his desk with one straight arm while he managed to hold the phone to his ear with the other. It was hard to breathe, hard to say anything at all. The handset creaked in his grip. "As far as I know, yes," he forced himself to say. "If I see her, I can tell her you called, but I'm not sure—"

"Are you him?" she asked.

The question was simple. Three basic words. But the answer eluded him entirely. Daniel closed his eyes, huffing three quick breaths through his nose, his jaw clenched tight. "Am I who, ma'am?"

"If you are, then you know *exactly* what I'm asking you, Mr. Marsden. Daniel. Are. You. Him?"

He lifted his flat hand from his desk, curled his fingers into his palm, and hit his knuckles against the wood, then shoved away from the desk as far as the corded phone would allow. "I would be," he confessed. "If I could be, ma'am. Yes, I know exactly what you're asking me."

"She's making a mistake," Tessa's mother said with as much conviction as if she'd known him forever. "I know in my heart she cares for Eddie, but she doesn't love him. Not the way she should love a husband. I can't convince her. Someone else has to."

He held his breath.

"*You* have to convince her, Daniel."

He released a shattered breath, one that drained him from his toes, and sniffed. "You seem a very insightful woman, Mrs. Spalaris. I would very much like to meet you one day."

"Do what you know is right, and I'll see you on Sunday for dinner."

She hung up without another word, and Daniel stared at the quiet phone in his hand. He thought the universe was sending him a message—give up on your false hopes—but what if he had the message all wrong? A rapid knock at his door jerked him back out of his stunned state. "Yeah," he called.

The door opened and Jillian came in, smiling. "We found her. Well, she just showed up again. Won't say where she's been for over two hours, but at least we don't have to call the cops. You were right."

He set the handset he still held back into the phone cradle. "I'm not always right," he said, managing only a jerked smile. "I try, though."

She gave him a funny look, then shook her head and hitched her thumb over her shoulder to indicate the hall, and what he assumed the activities beyond and in another part of his chapel. "Well, she's cleaning up—I don't know where she's been, but she looks like she had a hard time of it. Don't think I've ever seen anyone so petrified of getting married—and I've told Mr. Jackson she'd meet him in their designated chapel in..." She glanced at her watch. "Well, about now. Mark had to leave, so he couldn't stay to perform the ceremony after it was delayed, but Chris is here to officiate—Daniel?"

He didn't hear the rest after the single heartbeat that broke his resolve, kicked his better judgment to the curb, and threw his instincts into overdrive. Daniel rushed past Jillian into the hall and ran for the chapel wing.

Eddie looked back when Tessa opened the chapel door, stepping into the just shy of gaudy, vintage-decorated chapel. He had been speaking with the man standing at the altar, whom she assumed was the man designated to perform the ceremony, and now stared at her with wide, dark eyes.

"Oh, we weren't expecting you so quickly," the man said, stepping down from the podium. "Your witnesses should be here soon if you'd like to wait—"

"Eddie, I need to talk to you," she said quickly before she lost her nerve. Thank the universe for rushed packing, and the confidence instilled by a perfectly fitting red dress.

Eddie smiled, but there was no pleasure, no happiness in it. She'd known him too many years to be fooled. Tessa knew Edward Malcolm Jackson just as well as she knew herself. She knew his favorite color—blue—his favorite food—pork chops baked in spaghetti sauce—and knew he couldn't play an instrument to save his soul despite the five years of lessons his mother had paid for. She sat on the counter in his bathroom the first time he shaved the four spindly whiskers that had taken two weeks to grow on his chin and upper lip. He had helped her pick out bathing suits when she had nothing to fill them with and scoffed at her choices when she did. She knew his parents wanted him to be a lawyer, but he'd chosen finance instead, but they supported him. She knew everything.

She knew despite all that, as happy as she was to see him after it had been awhile, and as happy as she was to hear his voice when he gave her a call...her breath didn't catch and her pulse didn't jump when she thought of him.

Eddie looked to the officiant, who just nodded and stepped down, heading to a door along the side wall, saying he'd be back in a few minutes. Tessa gripped her hands behind her and walked to her best friend, and despite the pain in her heart, she felt strong. He reached a hand for her when she was close enough, and she took it without hesitation. When he pulled her to him for a hug, she wrapped her arms around his wide shoulders and hugged him back.

"It's okay," he said beside her ear. "I'm just glad to see you're okay. I was worried."

"I'm sorry," she said against the smooth fabric of his suit jacket. Right now she preferred soft tee shirts and worn jeans "I panicked and ran, and then didn't know how to come back and admit I was being foolish."

Eddie drew back and Tessa lowered her arms, resting them on his. She smiled, chastising herself for being such a fool. As soon as she was in the same room with her best friend, regardless of the circumstance, she felt better. Stronger. Maybe even wiser. He brought out the best in her. Always had.

"We've both been a bit foolish," Eddie said, sighing. He took her hand and kissed the back of it. "But I guess making drunk promises is pretty much the definition of foolish."

"I swore I'd never break a promise to you," she said, holding on tight to his hand.

"And you're not now." Before she could argue, he touched her chin so she'd look at him. "Tessa, the most important promise you ever made me was to be my best friend forever and ever and ever—"

"Plus a day," she said with a trembling voice, repeating the oath they'd made since she could remember.

He smiled wider and nodded. "I told my mother I would be the luckiest man in the world if I had you as a wife, and I still believe that would be true. You are an amazing woman, Tessa, and I'm so proud to have you in my life, but I'd rather have you as my best friend than know I'm responsible for stealing your happiness."

Before he could finish, Tessa was shaking her head. "No, Eddie."

"Shhh," he said, touching his finger to her lips. "I'm not going to make you say it. I've known since the morning after that night we made this stupid promise that it was wrong, and it wouldn't ever be right. I guess part of me did hope it might be, that it'd magically work." Resignation dragged down the deep timbre of his voice.

Tessa sucked in hard, wrapping her hands around his. "I do love you."

He smiled and leaned in to kiss her forehead. "I know you do. And I love you. But we both know it's not the right kind of love."

Tessa pressed her lips together and nodded, unable to say anything more. Every step to this room had been painful as she tried to figure out what she could say to Eddie to make this right, and in the end, he had saved her from it. Ever her best friend. She pushed up on her toes to wrap her arms around him again and let out a long, relieved sigh when he wrapped her in a firm, true, honest embrace.

Someone cleared their voice, and Tessa opened her eyes to see the minister or whatever title he held had returned to the chapel. He smiled and looked between them, hands folded in front of him. "Have we worked out everything? Are we ready?"

Before either Tessa or Eddie could answer, Daniel ran through the chapel doorway, the soles of his loafers sliding on the hardwood floor as he tried to stop. "Tessa!" he shouted.

For the first time all day, no guilt accompanied the warm flush on her skin when she saw Daniel Marsden. "Daniel, what is it?" she asked, taking a step back from Eddie.

"Who is this?" Eddie asked.

Daniel jogged into the chapel, out of breath. "I'm sorry. I know this makes me a total ass, but..." He shook his head, walking toward her, and with each step, Tessa's heart pounded faster. His smile grew on an exhale and he took her in from head to toe.

"But what?" she asked, moving away from Eddie and toward Daniel.

"But..." He smiled and shrugged, holding his hands away from him. A small chuckle laced his words. "But I've spent the last two hours knowing what I wish I could say to you, and now I can't think of any of it. Other than, damn, you are *stunning* in red."

"Tessa, who is this?" Eddie asked again, his voice firmer with the demand.

She laughed softly, not looking away from Daniel, and laid her palm on Eddie's arm. "That's Daniel Marsden, owner of the First, Last, Everything wedding chapel."

"What?" Eddie declared.

Tessa shook her head and took another step toward Daniel. "I'll explain everything. I promise, but right now—"

She didn't get to finish. Daniel matched her step and made it to her in two long strides, taking her head in his hands before he touched her in any other way. She had only a second to take a breath before his open mouth covered hers and all thought flew away in a kiss that instantly turned her lower stomach into a horde of butter-flies, her blood into champagne, and electrified her skin. A low purr she knew she should probably be embarrassed about hummed from her throat, but it only seemed to ignite him more. Not that she was complaining.

Daniel slid a hand behind her head, supporting her as he wrapped his arm around her and held her as close as she'd wanted him to all day. Never had she been kissed with such intent, like he needed every moment as much as she did. When his tongue slid across hers with seductive ease, everything liquefied and her knees nearly gave beneath her. But he held her, and kissed her, and left absolutely no doubt this...*this*...was the lightning bolt her mother always told her about.

Tessa held on to him, her arms wrapped around his sides, and he again laid his hands along the side of her face, holding her so she couldn't move too far away, their rapid breaths mingling between them. Daniel's eyes were half-closed, his focus on her mouth, his lips teasing to kiss again as he brushed his nose along hers.

"That wasn't anything like I imagined it would be," he said with a breath, his kiss-slick lips curling up in a smile that left her devastated. "I never could have imagined that."

She shook her head as much as she could in his hold and tipped up her chin to draw another kiss from him.

"Don't marry him, Tessa," he begged, looking her in the eyes, all teasing gone.

She smiled and laughed. "I wasn't going to anyway."

Daniel let her go only the second needed to wrap her in his arms and lift her off the ground, capturing her lips again in a life-changing kiss.

Chapter Six

"I knew you'd look amazing in red."

Daniel glanced across the space of his car at the most beautiful woman he had ever seen. She leaned her temple against the back of the seat, watching him, and he lifted their joined hands to kiss the back of hers before focusing again on the road. Didn't matter if he looked at her, or not, she was infused into his mind. Her rich brown hair no longer had the forced salon curl to it, but hung around her shoulders in soft waves, and although the striking starlet makeup had made his breath catch, her simple makeup was far more appealing to him. She was more exotic in her simplicity than the themed mask she'd worn earlier that day. Dark eyes, rich skin, beautiful, all made irresistible in a simple red dress that left her arms bare, fitted snug to her torso, and hung loose around her hips and legs. He wanted to know more, learn more, study her until he knew every curve and line by memory.

The idea made it hard to focus, uncomfortable to sit, and he had to talk himself out of turning around and heading back to his apartment rather than his mother's house. Part of him wanted to share her with everyone he loved, and part of him wanted to keep her all to himself.

"When I opened my suitcase and saw it on top, it was like the universe was giving me one more nudge toward you." She lifted her head off the headrest. "Is that crazy?"

Daniel laughed out loud, glancing into his side mirror to check if he could merge left and get around the slow moving truck in front of him. For the first time in as long as he could remember, he was anxious to get home. They were running late, but it couldn't be helped. He knew his mother would have plenty to say, but nothing—*nothing*—could bring him down today. "Not any crazier than anything else that has happened in the last few hours."

She smiled, and the effect on him was instant, complete, and far too distracting. He had to make himself pay attention to the road, and was insanely happy right then that he drove an automatic and didn't have to let go of her hand to shift. Still holding his hand, she twisted to pull up her knees and tuck her feet into the seat, all while managing to remain buckled in, giving him an enticing view of her legs peeking out from beneath the hem of her red dress.

The next few hours might be the longest in his life.

"How long until we get there?" she asked.

"Maybe ten minutes, depending on traffic."

"How long do we have to stay?" The husky curl of her voice made his blood rush, and he looked her way, immediately hit by the dark, enticing warmth in her eyes.

Daniel swallowed and licked his lips before focusing on the road again. "Tempt me too much and we'll go home right now."

She let out a long sigh, relaxing into the seat again. "I don't suppose that would be the best first impression, hmm?"

Before he could answer, Tessa's phone buzzed in the drink holder between the seats, and she let go of his hand to pick it up. Daniel took the moment to grip the steering wheel with both hands and navigate a bit more aggressively through the traffic heading out of Vegas to

Henderson. It wasn't a long drive, but tonight it felt like an eternity. It was a text because he glanced sideways to see her smiling as she read the screen.

"It's Mom," she said, peeking at him over the phone. She then held up the phone, aiming at him. "Smile."

He did, taking a second to glance at her and the phone clicked when she took a picture. She went back to texting. "She wants to know what you look like," she explained as she texted.

"Hope I don't disappoint."

Tessa chuckled, then laughed out loud. "She says you're a hottie, and good taste in men run in the family."

Daniel smiled, but a moment of concern dimmed his elated mood. He looked to the side mirror and pulled into traffic again, moving past a twenty-year-old Nissan.

"What's wrong?" Tessa asked.

"Nothing," he answered quickly, winking at her.

Tessa shifted so she sat forward, her knees tucked against the center console, and leaned on the armrest between them. "No, you just thought something."

Taking a moment longer than probably safe, he stared down at her and the apprehension eased. He smiled and reached for her hand again. "I have a hard time believing your parents will be okay with this. I mean, you left for Vegas with the intent of marrying Eddie—"

"And even if I don't like to admit they were right, they were right. I didn't belong with Eddie."

"I don't disagree, but—"

"But nothing. They're okay. I promise."

He brought her hand to his lips and kissed it because kissing her the way he wanted wasn't an option until they got to Mom's. Well, even then, kissing her the way he wanted wasn't an option, but he could at least get a fix. He'd left the chapel figuring the 215 was the best route, not that any would be good this time of day, but right now he cursed traffic.

"Besides, they'll get to know you this weekend."

That made him smile, but a smile had been firmly attached to his face since that afternoon when she said she wasn't marrying Eddie and had only varied by degrees between permanent and cheek-aching. Five and a half hours ago, he'd walked into his office to find a beautiful woman in tears. Three and a half hours ago, he'd begged her not to marry another man. Since then, many things had been discussed, many plans made, and some executed. Tomorrow morning he was leaving Vegas with Tessa to head back to Los Angeles, but only long enough for her to give her boss notice and arrange to have her things packed and shipped back to Nevada.

No hesitation. No turning back.

They were doing this. They'd *done* this.

They reached Lake Mead Parkway and traffic slowed with the reduced speed limit, but also thinned, and anticipation bubbled in his veins.

"We're almost there."

She tightened her grip on his hand. "Okay, now I'm the nervous one. At least you have a couple of days to prepare, and by what I gather, your parents aren't exactly the spontaneous type."

"Granted," he said, turning onto his mother's street, an older area of Henderson and the same street on which he had grown up. The trees were taller here, and more of them than in some of the newer developments, the benefit of decades of growth behind them. Mom's house was a modest ranch, cast in shade by the large tree in the front yard. As they approached, he noted both his father's SUV and his sister Rebecca's blue Prius. Horace would have come with her.

"Hail, hail, the gang's all here," he said as he maneuvered into a parallel parking spot behind his father's vehicle under the shade of the neighbor's tree.

Putting the car in park, he jumped out and ran around to Tessa's side, reaching her door just as she opened it. He offered his hand as she unfolded herself from her contorted position and slipped her feet into the sandals she'd discarded on the passenger's side floor. As she stood free of the car, Daniel tugged her toward him, shut the door, and leaned her back against the side of the car, delving in for a kiss he put his full focus into because it'd be a while before he'd have a chance at another.

Unless he managed to sneak her away to his old bedroom for a few minutes. The idea made him smile into the kiss.

Tessa raised her arms to draw him close, and pushed her fingers into his hair, and the sensation was gasoline on a fire. Daniel moaned into the kiss and curled his hands into the material of her skirt around her hips, the urge—the *need*—to know the feel of her skin almost undeniable. Tessa shifted in his embrace, angling her body against him, and he nearly came undone.

"It's about time you showed up, Danny. Mom hasn't stopped with the list of—Oh, geez!"

Tessa stilled in his hold, her fingers relaxing their play in his hair, and Daniel smiled against her lips before offering one final, quick kiss and withdrawing. Unwilling to let her go yet, he kept his arm around her waist so she was against his side, and looked into her wide, panicked eyes before turning them both to face his sister.

"Hey, Rebecca," he said, purposefully sounding as nonchalant as possible.

His little sister stared at him with her arms crossed, her hip cocked, and her eyebrows arched high. "Hey, Rebecca?" she parroted. "I find you making out in the street, leaving me alone in the house— an *hour* late for dinner—with Mom and Dad tag teaming Horace and me, and all you say is *hey, Rebecca?*"

Daniel slid his palm across Tessa's back to her arm, and down until he could lace their hands together while taking steps away from the car. She followed but raised her other hand to run her fingertips over her lips and smooth her hair. When he reached his sister, he leaned down to kiss her cheek.

"Yep," was all he said.

Rebecca scowled at him, but turned a curious look on Tessa,

extending her hand. Tessa had to let go of his to take it. "Rebecca Marsden."

"Tessa," she said, glancing quickly at Daniel.

He grinned and found her hand again as soon as his sister released her. "You ready?"

Tessa laughed nervously but nodded. "Sure. The day isn't over yet, right?"

Rebecca still gave them a curious look as she led the way toward the house. "Did Mom know you were bringing a guest?"

"Even *I* didn't know last time we talked," he admitted.

Her scowl deepened. "You're grinning like a fool."

Daniel looked to Tessa, and the hint of a smirk on her lips bloomed warm in his chest. He lifted their joined hands and kissed her fingers. "Fools rush in. Isn't that the song?" Tessa nodded, and he felt some of her nervous tension ease.

"Whatever," Rebecca mumbled, opening the door to the house.

Voices carried from the dining room, and the air smelled of roast chicken and au gratin potatoes. Each voice was distinctive: Mom, Dad, his stepmother Stacy, and Horace, Rebecca's fiancé. Engagement was the topic of discussion.

"See what I mean?" Rebecca said, leading the way toward the small dining room. "You've left us here for slaughter."

"Don't worry, sis," Daniel said, setting his hand on his sister's shoulder just short of entering the dining room. "In a few minutes, I guarantee you and Horace will no longer be the topic of discussion."

Tessa's grip on his hand firmed, and he winked at her.

"Rebecca, will you stay out here with Tessa for a minute? I'd rather get past the initial deluge before I submit her to it."

"Um, sure..."

"Daniel," Tessa said softly, her grip tightening when he tried to step away.

He stayed behind the wall that hid him from the view of his family and turned to Tessa, bringing his free hand to her cheek so he could hold her when he leaned in for a kiss. She pressed her palm to his chest, and all blood rushed to that spot to be closer to her touch. Unable to take too long, he ended the longer kiss with a short punctuation, then let go and stepped into the dining room.

As soon as Daniel was out of sight, Tessa's blood went cold and her pulse practically vibrated it went so fast, making her dizzy. She stepped back, her hands behind her, until she touched the wall and leaned against it with her eyes closed and her head down, trying to meter her breathing. His sister touched her arm.

"Hey, you okay?"

All she could do was nod. Right up until now—until this moment—she had thought they were a little crazy for what they'd done, but now she was pretty sure they were certifiably insane.

"Danny," came a woman's voice, followed by a scrape of chair legs. "We were beginning to worry."

"I left a message saying I'd be a little late," Daniel explained, and the soft sound of a kiss, probably on his mother's cheek, carried to the hallway.

She raised her head and opened her eyes, meeting the curious gaze of his sister. Even if she hadn't seen the picture in his office, she would have seen the family resemblance. She was just a shorter and more feminine version of Daniel. Tessa tried to smile but felt too shaky to carry it off. The "what if" scenarios suddenly decided to all play out at once.

"Was it because of that issue that came up while we were on the phone?" his mother asked.

Daniel laughed. "Yeah, something like that. Hi, Dad. Stacy. Horace."

A man cleared his throat. "Did you see your sister? She thought you had arrived and went to check."

"That's my father," Rebecca whispered. Tessa nodded.

"Ah, yeah. She's around here somewhere. I saw her."

"Are you going to sit down?" his father asked. "Now that you're here, we can discuss this foolishness about your sister getting married. No insult to you, Horace. We like you well enough, but there's no need to rush things."

"We've been together long enough to know, Mr. Marsden," said another man. By the smile that immediately graced Rebecca's face, Tessa assumed that was her fiancé. "We are sure, and we aren't rushing."

"Danny..." his mother led, her voice pleading.

Daniel's chuckle preceded his answer. "I don't think I'm the one to convince Rebecca and Horace of anything," he said, his smile carrying in his voice.

"Danny, sit down, for goodness sake," his mother said.

"Just a second, Ma, I promise. I want to let you know I'm going out of town for a couple of weeks. I'm leaving tomorrow."

"Why?" his mother exclaimed. "Is something wrong? Where are you going?"

"Something very important has come up," Daniel explained, and Tessa had to press a hand to her chest to keep her heart from pounding through her ribs. "Absolutely nothing is wrong. I'm going to Los Angeles, but we'll be back in a couple of weeks."

"We?" his mother asked. "Who is going with you?"

"Hang on to that question," Daniel said, and his footfalls carried as he came toward the hall.

Tessa pushed herself away from the wall when he came into view and reached for him as soon as he was close enough, gripping his arms. He kissed her forehead, then nodded to his sister so that she could go in. She shrugged and left them, and the hum of conversation was lost on Tessa through the pounding in her ears.

Daniel wrapped her in his arms and she pressed her cheek to his chest, finding some satisfaction in the fact his heart pounded as fast as hers. "I love you," he whispered. "Just in case you weren't sure, I thought I should mention it again."

She laughed at his teasing and attempt at soothing her rioting nerves and nodded against his tee shirt. "I sure hope so," she said softly. "I love you, too, Daniel."

He pulled back and took her face in his hands, kissing her lips.

"Danny?" his mother called. "Where did you go?" Her chair legs scraped on the floor. "I'll go look—"

"I'm coming right in, Ma," he called back. "We're coming."

"Who is he talking about?" came a woman's voice Tessa didn't recognize, and she had to assume it was Stacy, Daniel's stepmother. "Rebecca, is someone out there with him? Who is it?"

"Your guess is as good as mine," Rebecca answered.

One more kiss and Daniel laced their fingers. She stood as close to his side as she could, gripping his arm with her free hand, and resolved her nerve to walk with him. After everything else she'd done today, this should be easy.

Right?

They walked around the corner into the small dining room, and four sets of eyes turned on them. She recognized them all from the photo, except the woman seated beside Daniel's mother. She was perhaps slightly younger than Mr. Marsden, with dyed blond hair curling under at her shoulders and warm green eyes. She gaped, as surprised as the rest of them when they came into view, especially Daniel's mother, who stared at them with wide eyes and a slack jaw.

"Mom, Dad, everyone. This is Tessa."

She held her breath. Unable to watch their reactions, she tightened her grip on Daniel's hand and stared only at him. He turned his focus on her, smiling down at her so wide his dimples showed. At that moment, whatever they said, whatever they did, it didn't matter. As long as he looked at her like that for the rest of their lives.

He bent his arm and lifted their joined hands. His right. Her left. And stared down at the ring on her second finger. They would have been to the house sooner, but he'd insisted they do things as right as possible. He brought the hand to his lips and kissed her finger over the simple gold band.

"Theresa Spalaris Marsden." He sighed, and the way he smiled wider made Tessa's eyes well and her heart swell. "My wife."

Chaos ensued...but she didn't care.

My wife.

The Beginning...

About the Author

 Gail R. Delaney is a multi-published, award-winning author of romance in multiple sub-genres, including contemporary romance, romantic suspense, and epic science fiction romance. She always wrote stories as a kid through her teens, but didn't decide to write 'for publication' until her early twenties after the death of her mother. While helping her father go through her mother's papers, she found a box her mother kept with everything Gail had ever written—from book reports to short stories. It was then she realized her mother saw her as a writer, and it was time to live up to her mother's vision.

You can find out more about Gail R. Delaney's body of work at:

http://www.GailDelaney.com

Also by Gail R. Delaney

Contemporary Romance

Something Better

Precious Things

Feel My Love

Baker Street Legacy

Book One: My Dear Branson

Book Two: The Empty Chair

Book Three: Indefinite Doubt

Coming Soon

<u>THE FUTURE POSSIBLE SAGA</u>

PART ONE: THE PHOENIX REBELLION

BOOK ONE: REVOLUTION

BOOK TWO: OUTCASTS

BOOK THREE: GAINING GROUND

BOOK FOUR: END GAME

PART TWO: PHOENIX RISING

BOOK ONE: JANUS

BOOK TWO: TRIAD

BOOK THREE: STASIS

Book Four: Liber

Something Better

A world-renowned author and an A-list actor fell in love. Sounds like a RomCom movie plot but may just be their happily ever after. Cue the villain plot twist...

Andrea Parker has made a career out of romance, except the only romance in her life is the kind between the pages of a book; and now on the big screen when her best-selling novels are adapted to film.

David Bishop's face – and okay, yeah, much of his body – is known worldwide as the Hottest Bachelor in Hollywood. But just like most of the rest of the world, he is smitten with the brilliant and talented author Andi Parker. Little does he know the easy part will be convincing her to give him a chance.

Andi is a divorced, single mom with enough years between her and David Bishop to make her wonder what he sees. But David is nothing if not committed to showing her he's more than just a handsome face.

She's ready to believe there might be something better waiting for her, then enters the *dastardly bastardly* villain in the form of her ex-husband to screw up their potential Happily Ever After.

Something Better

Preview of Chapter One

"I'm sorry," David said softly, roughening his voice to give it weight and sincerity. He laid his palm against Taylor's cheek and leaned forward until their foreheads touched.

Too quickly, she pulled away and tipped her head back to look at him. She shook her head, her forehead creasing. "For what?"

He tried again to make contact, touching her cheek. "For not coming home when I promised you I would. For not being here when you needed me. For not being here when—"

"Stop," she snapped, cutting off any explanation he could offer.

He brought both hands up to touch her face, brushing over her lipstick-slick lower lip with his thumb.

"I'm sorry—" The rest went unfinished when Taylor arched up on her toes and threw her arms around his neck. He managed a quick mumble against her lips before she kissed him, her fingers pushing impatiently into his hair.

A low-but-definitely-feminine groan, laced with "Oh, for pity's sake," echoed through the soundstage just before the Director's loud voice drowned it out.

"Cut!"

David detangled himself from Taylor and took a step back, running the side of his finger over his lips to remove any lipstick she'd left behind. The air in the studio was hot, and he'd been under the lights too long because irritation licked at a spot between his shoulder blades, making him even more tense and aggravated. Like he wasn't frustrated enough with Taylor, although he'd never say it.

"What?" Taylor huffed, stepping back from her mark. "What was wrong this time, Benton?"

Benton stepped into the circle of light, his features crinkled and pulled tight with tension. David understood Benton, as director, felt the pinch as much as anyone. Maybe more, because time was money and no one knew better than the man in charge on set. The more times they had to reshoot the further behind they got. "Taylor-Sweet-heart-Darling...we've gone over this. We all know just how kissable David is—"

David fought the urge to roll his eyes and took a bottle of cold water offered to him by one of the PAs, snapping the cap open before draining half the bottle.

"But, you need to listen to me on this one, honey. This scene is about..." Benton trailed off, holding his hands out as if silently pleading for Taylor to understand. "It's about..."

"It's about coming home," Andi Parker said from the shadows.

David watched her step into the light, and not for the first time since he met her, he enjoyed the flash of heat skimming just below the surface of his skin. Andrea Parker was not only gifted—he hadn't been able to put her books down once he'd been cast for the movie adaptation—but she was one of the most beautiful women he had ever seen. No...correct that. She was *the* most beautiful woman he'd ever seen.

No more than five-foot-three, she was fair-skinned with sun-touched red hair and a row of freckles across the bridge of her nose just begging to be caressed. She had the curve and shape of a woman —not like stick-figure Barbie imitators he saw in Hollywood most of the time—and a dry wit that kept him laughing most of the time when they had the chance to talk. Her jokes were always subtle and delivered in a single shot, and if you weren't paying attention it was lost on you all together.

That was her nature...if you weren't looking, she could slip into a room unnoticed. Just as easily, she could be the only person in a studio full of people.

Today she wore a simple, yellow sundress with tiny flowers scattered on it that buttoned down the front from the 'v' of her neckline to the hemline falling just a couple of inches above her knees. The fabric looked soft and warm and draped down her in a way that made him want to lay his hands at her waist, just to see what she felt like. Her short hair flipped and curled around her face, and he wondered sometimes if it just *happened* that way, or if she worked at it. Small, oval glasses perched on her nose, the dark frames making her red hair seem even richer. But, today she wasn't smiling...and David had a good idea why.

They'd been working on this single scene all morning. Benton had tried to tell Taylor what he wanted from nearly every direction: left, right, over, and under. Regardless, Taylor had done the same thing with each take—well, with some variation to show she was at least trying. Taylor seemed to have her mind set on this scene happening a certain way and didn't want to give it up. She'd impressed David with her performance in other scenes; nailing them with such emotion and skill it often only took a shot or two to get every angle and delivery they needed.

But this one scene seemed to have her stumped.

Until this last shot, Andi had stayed quiet and left the directing to Benton. The two of them—Writer and Director—were almost always on the same page when it came to the interpretation of a scene. It surprised David now that she would be so vocal.

Not that he minded...he liked her voice. She was soft-spoken with a lilt to her voice and a delicate accent he hadn't ever been able to place. He hid his smile behind the mouth of his water bottle.

"It's about forgiveness, and it's about realizing what you've got...

and being *thankful* for second chances." She stopped a few feet from them, crossing her arms. "It's *not* about sex."

"It's about intimacy," Benton tag-teamed.

"Exactly," Andi declared loudly. "It's about intimacy. You can't—" Andi waved her hands in the air, her cheeks flushing. She motioned toward David, her bright eyes settling on him for only a brief moment. "—latch onto him like he's some kind of life preserver or the air tube to your oxygen tank. Let *him* come to *you*. You're in shock. You're exhausted. You're thankful he's alive, but you have to be tentative."

"Yeah, but wouldn't it be hotter if we're all...you know...excited?"

Without answering, Andi crossed the short space and took Taylor's spot at the mark. Her small hand settled on David's arm, and he immediately felt the heat as the touch snapped his attention to her.

"You're frightening me, Jason."

Without looking to his right, David handed off the half-empty bottle of water and took his spot. He laid his hand over hers and curled his fingers slightly. Her skin was warm and her hand was delicate in his hold.

"Don't be. I'm okay. Now." He smiled, just slightly. "I wasn't, but I am now."

Andi stared at their hands and drew in a shaky breath. When she looked up again, David shifted his stance to face her straight. "I'm sorry," he said softly. Just as he had before, he leaned forward until their foreheads touched. Taylor was taller and he had to bend his knees slightly to bring himself more level with Andi, but he liked the way it aligned their bodies. Her eyes fluttered closed and she raised her chin, bringing their lips closer together without touching.

"For what?" Andi asked, speaking naturally as Anna, his character's wife. Her fingers curled around his wrist and her breath skimmed across his chin, but she didn't pull back or open her eyes.

"For not coming home when I promised you I would. For not being here when you needed me. For not being here when—"

"Stop," she said in barely a whisper. Only then did she open her eyes and tip her head back enough to look at him.

He brought both hands up to touch her face, brushing her lower lip with his thumb. It was slick and smooth, like she may have just applied lip balm, and the idea tugged at something somewhere between his chest and his gut. He bit down for a moment. *Jason would love the feel of his wife's lips after so long...*

"I'm sorry I forgot," he forced out, finishing the line this time. He paused and swallowed, leaning closer to her until their lips almost touched. Her breath was quick and shallow. "How could I forget you?"

The scene said THEY KISSED SOFTLY, but David hesitated. She wasn't an actress, and he doubted she'd initiate the scene with the intent of carrying it this far. Then Andi leaned into him, her body tilting to press against his chest and he took one hand from her cheek to lace it into her hair, soft curls wrapping around his fingers like ribbons of silk.

She gasped softly before he pressed their lips together. He couldn't force himself to take a breath as they held that position, and he swore he could hear the pounding of her heart. Andi played the part just as he imagined, her body shaking slightly in his embrace. Her lips parted as he pulled back a degree, and he kissed her again, letting his tongue skim along the edge of her lips.

Her fingers curled into the front of his shirt, and her head tilted slightly to the side to effectively deepen the kiss. David loosened his fingers from her hair, sliding his hand back to her cheek as he broke contact. Despite himself, he returned for one final, brief kiss before withdrawing. Andi's body swayed with his, but she righted herself on her feet and her eyes fluttered open. Bright color stained her cheeks, and she blinked rapidly.

Andi looked up at him, her face flushed and warm beneath his touch, and she blinked several times. Swallowing, David pulled his attention away from her face to look at Benton.

"That what you want?"

At first, he was met by silence. Benton stood at the edge of the light, his hands hanging limp at his side and his mouth open. Taylor stood beside him, mimicking his look of shock as she fanned herself with one hand. Even the PA who now held David's half-empty bottle of water stared wide-eyed.

Benton nodded. That was the only answer David got. He looked back down at Andi and realized he had begun stroking her cheek with his thumb.

She blinked again and licked her lips, turning away. Then with just as much skill as any actor David had ever seen, Andi took in a long, steadying breath and closed her eyes. When she opened them again, her voice was steady and the flush had lightened in her cheeks.

"Perfect," she said with a lopsided grin and made a thumbs-up. "You nailed it." She turned to Benton and Taylor, stepping away from him. "I'll be back in a few minutes."

When she brushed past him, David couldn't fight the urge to turn his hand so their fingertips brushed across each other. Her attention never wavered, but David thought maybe her hand angled back to him before the contact broke and she stepped over the mangle of cables and wires to disappear into the darkness of the soundstage.

Benton cleared his throat. "Yeah. Let's do that again."

Taylor stepped to him with a wide smile, looking up at him through her mascara-thickened lashes. She said something, but David's attention had followed Andi in the darkness and he didn't bring himself back to the moment until he no longer heard the soft pad of her sandals on the concrete.

With a performance like that, she belongs in front of the camera, not behind a computer.

Andi tripped taking the two little steps into her trailer. "Ow!" She winced at the sharp pain in her left knee. "That's gonna leave a mark,"

she mumbled as she opened the door and escaped to the dark interior of the small space she called her own when she visited the set.

Her heart pounded so hard in her chest that each beat thrummed at her temples. She was hot everywhere. Most people flushed in their cheeks, but she swore the heat beneath her skin spread from her red hair to her red-painted toenails. She thanked God for the small refrigerator in her trailer stocked with cold Diet Coke. As soon as she curled her fingers around the cold can, she pressed the metal to the base of her throat, gasping at the near-burn against her flushed skin. She shifted the can to her cheek and forehead before sitting at the tiny, Formica-covered table nestled into the front of the trailer.

Andi set her elbow on the tabletop and leaned her burning forehead into her hand, expelling a shaky breath. "Get a grip, Andrea," she scolded herself in the silent trailer.

But the only thought that would register in her brain was *Wow!* Right alongside *Holy Cannoli!* It had been a long time, longer than Andi would admit to anyone except maybe Maggie, since something as simple as a kiss had melted her insides into a bucket of girly goo. Years probably...*how pathetic is that?*

"He's an actor," she mumbled, finally popping open the Diet Coke. "It's his *job* to sell the kiss, right? Right. So...that's why he got the job. He's good." Andi rolled her eyes. "Good doesn't even begin to cover it."

Her cell phone rang and she picked it up from the table where she'd left it that morning—always afraid it would go off during filming —and smiled when she saw the name on the screen.

Andi was quite proud her voice didn't quiver when she answered. "Hey, Mags."

"Hey..." Maggie, Andi's literary agent and dearest friend on the planet paused on the other end. "What's wrong?"

Typical of Maggie, all she had to hear was Andi's voice to know something was wrong...okay, so not wrong...just...*No, definitely wrong!* "What makes you think anything is wrong?"

"Oh, please. Spill."

"*Nothing* is *wrong*...really."

"Do I *have* to come hurt you?"

Andi laughed, feeling some of the tension David's kiss had created releasing enough she could drop her shoulders and take a sip of her soda. The cold, crispness eased her throat and spread out in her chest, relieving some of the flush. She drew in a long, metered breath through her nose in an attempt to calm herself further, but realized quickly *that* was a mistake.

The scent of David Bishop clung to her clothes and filled her senses. Just like that—*BAM*—the flush was back. *You're insane, Andrea Parker! Certifiable!*

"I swear, Andi...I'm catching the next plane..."

"Okay, okay. Relax." Andi took a deep breath. "Something just happened on set that has me...um...frazzled." *And hot...and bothered... and apparently insane.*

Maggie huffed on the other end of the line. "I told you, Andi...you can't agonize over every little nuance of every scene. Let Benton direct. The two of you usually see things the same, and—"

"No, it's nothing like that," Andi said, gently cutting Mags off before she went on a rant. Andi quickly explained which scene they had been filming, and the ongoing trouble with Taylor wanting to attach herself to David like some freaky succubus. She took another long drink before finishing the story with, "So, I showed her what I wanted."

There was a silent pause on the other end of the line, and Andi could almost hear Maggie's wheels churning. "You..."

"Yep," Andi answered before Maggie finished the question, popping the 'p' loudly through her recently-David-kissed lips. *Oh, Mama...*

"Aaaand..."

"And I'm hiding in my trailer, sucking down a cold Diet Coke, and wondering just how small that upright coffin they call a shower is in my tiny bathroom—because I could use a cold dousing right about now."

Andi sat and drank her soda in silence for the next two minutes while Maggie first laughed herself breathless, then tried to speak again. When it sounded like Maggie might have herself under control, Andi sighed. "Are you done now?"

There was another loud snort. "Nope, don't think so."

A soft knock at the trailer door stopped Andi from saying something back. "Someone is here, hang on."

"Maybe it's David. He wants to rehearse."

"Not funny. Come on in," she called toward the door. Then anything else she might have said to Maggie froze in her throat when the door opened and David stuck his head inside. Her hand holding the phone slid away from her face, and Maggie's voice grew distant.

"If the trailer's rockin'..." she heard faintly.

David smiled as he took the steps—much more gracefully than she had managed just minutes before—into her trailer. "Hi," he said simply.

"Hi..." Andi managed, already feeling the heat blooming in her cheeks like a California wildfire. Then she heard Maggie calling out her name, and she put the phone back to her ear. "I'll call you later, 'kay?"

"Who is it?"

"I'll call you."

"It's him."

David's mouth tipped into a quick, sexy grin and with it, an all-new flash of heat spreading from her throat to her cheeks, Andi realized her penchant for keeping her phone volume high had let him hear at least the tail end of her conversation.

"I'll call you later, Mags."

"Don't you hang up on me, Andrea Parker," Maggie shouted just before Andi snapped the phone shut and set it down on the table beside her now painfully empty Diet Coke.

"Problem?" David asked with a slight lilt to his voice.

Andi shook her head. "Nope. What's up?"

"Benton called lunch," David said, closing the door behind him as he took the last step into the trailer. Suddenly, the trailer seemed not just small, but microscopic.

The idea of food made Andi's stomach flip. She yanked her hands back from the tabletop and stuck them underneath, clenching them together in her lap. "Okay." One thing Andi had always managed to do, no matter how intimidated or nervous she was, was to meet someone's eyes when she spoke to them. Her father had taught her no matter what was going on in her head if she could look someone in the eye, they'd respect her.

Right now, she could barely manage to glance up from the speckled tabletop to make polite conversation. Any second now, she knew she was going to burst into flame and leave behind nothing more than a pile of ash and a pair of glasses.

"We finished the scene. Benton said you should see it before he calls it."

Andi shook her head. "I'm sure it's fine this time."

"I think it's what you want..." His voice trailed off.

She cleared her throat and nodded, flipping a bit of hair behind her ear so it didn't touch her cheek. "I'll check it after lunch."

"You'll like it."

Andi snapped her gaze to him, and her heart jumped straight into her throat. Where had the weeks of comfortable camaraderie gone? Of sitting at the picnic tables outside during lunch and talking? Him laughing politely at her lame attempts at humor? It wasn't like she didn't *know* he was sex-on-legs, she wasn't blind or stupid. And although her social life in the last few years resembled the life of a nun, she wasn't *actually* celibate. Not by choice, anyway. David Bishop was six-plus feet of hotness with thick brown hair with just enough natural wave for running her fingers through, and eyes that crinkled just right at the corners to show he laughed a lot.

Why was it thirty-year-old men could have laugh lines and it was sexy, but thirty-*ahem*-something women couldn't have a single line without looking haggard? The cosmos wasn't fair.

Andi blinked away the random thought and nervously took one

hand from under the table to pick up her empty can, tapping it with a hollow thud against the table. "Good," she managed to say.

David shifted his stance, pushing his hands into the front pockets of his jeans. In an attempt to calm her nerves, Andi drew in a slow breath—which usually worked—except now it wasn't just her clothes that smelled of him, but the entire space. It wasn't an overpowering smell like someone bathed in aftershave, but a subtle mingling of sandalwood and fresh air.

There you go, Andi...waxing poetic again. How exactly does one 'smell' like fresh air?

"Did you ever consider acting?" David asked, his voice in the silence making her jump.

Andi chuckled and shook her head. "No. I can't act."

"Really..." he said slowly, pulling the word out with a slight quirk at the corner of his mouth. His voice was rough and heavy, practically sitting in the air between them. Andi managed to force herself to meet his gaze. He swallowed and she watched the slow bob of his Adam's apple.

Her heart pounded so hard in her chest, she felt each pulse thunder in her ears, and each breath she took echoed like she had her head in a barrel. That little quirk of his mouth turned into a slow grin.

Stop it!

"No," she reiterated. She turned her attention again to the speckled Formica, digging her nail into a nick. "No acting, just..." Despite her resolve to memorize the pattern, she looked up again and found him staring at her. Her throat was suddenly as dry as the Mojave, and she wished more than anything there was one final swallow of Diet Coke left. "I just...I know how it's supposed to be."

He took a step toward her, and suddenly Andi couldn't sit at the tiny table anymore—or share the tiny space—or apparently use her feet properly. She stumbled sideways, attempting to grip the table edge to keep herself from falling, but it was David's hands that caught her. His long fingers curled around her bare arm, and Andi stared down at the contact, unable to look away as his other hand settled at her waist. The shift of her cotton dress over her skin almost made her shiver. As she watched, his fingers relaxed and slid over her skin up her arm to her shoulder. She had to close her eyes, and chant silently in her head.

You're insane, Andrea! Insane and aroused! But mostly insane! Stop it! Just stop it already!

"Andi—"

"I sh-should go check the shot," she rambled, trying to move past him before she made a total and complete fool of herself. *Yeah, like you haven't already.* "I don't want to hold up Benton."

"Andi..." he said again. His hand left her waist to block her escape. Just like he had with the first, he let his fingers brush her skin at the elbow then slide slowly up her bare arm.

A shiver danced up her spine, and she bit back a groan. His hand continued along her shoulder to her throat, his fingertip pausing at her pulse point. Now there was no doubt he knew how hard her heart pounded with him this close. David nudged her chin with his thumb, urging her to tip her head slightly away from him, elongating the side of her neck. He stepped closer and leaned in until the rough bristle of his whiskers brushed her cheek and his breath warmed her skin.

"When you said those lines, and you shook when I touched you, you made me believe you were Anna and I was Jason." His voice was so low she wouldn't have been able to hear him if he hadn't been so close. The timbre vibrated against the side of her throat, and she had to force her eyes from fluttering closed. "And when I kissed you, I felt it. I really *felt* it."

Andi had to close her eyes to keep herself from getting dizzy. *This is one of those vivid dreams of yours, Andrea. That's all. Just a vivid dream. Any second now, your alarm is going to go off and you're going to have to drag yourself out of bed.*

Yep...any second now.

David slid his cheek along hers, tilting his head so their lips hovered against each other. Andi tried not to breathe, but it only made her head swim more. She sucked in oxygen, and her senses filled with David Bishop. His thumb stroked along her jaw and down her throat to the hollow of her collarbone, and even with her eyes closed, she knew he watched her for every reaction. Andi tried to take a step back, but the table was too close and she bumped her bottom against it, her fingers instinctively curling around the edge.

"I want to know something..." David said, his words trailing off unfinished.

"Wh-what?" she managed to ask, and when she spoke, her lips brushed against his and her breath hitched. She wanted to lick her lips, but she was afraid—*no, more like terrified*—her tongue would wet more than her own lips. He was so close.

"I wonder..." His pause finally piqued her curiosity so much she opened her eyes, and gasped. David's face wasn't an inch from hers and his gray-blue eyes watched her intently. "I wonder if I kissed you now—not as Jason and Anna, but David and Andi—would it feel the same?"

Andi shook her head slightly, the first action to come to her muddled brain. His thumbs rubbed across her throat and she swallowed hard.

"Or would it be better?"

"No," she managed to say.

He tipped his chin so it nudged hers. "You don't think so. Are you sure?"

"No," she parroted.

David smiled, and took his hands from her throat to lay his palms against her cheeks. His mouth hovered over hers, his breath warm. When the tip of his tongue touched her lower lip, Andi gasped as a bolt of awareness struck her, shooting down her spine to her stomach like an electrified lightning rod. Before she could finish drawing her breath, his mouth covered hers.

And then he was kissing her without restraint or temperance, and everything inside her liquefied. Andi had to grab hold of his shirt, curling her fingers into the soft cotton behind his shoulders just to hold her feet, and his hands shifted to her back, pulling her closer to him. She whimpered, and mentally groaned because it had to be the unsexiest sound ever heard. But his hold tightened on her, pressing her so close to him it was hard to draw breath into her lungs.

Not that she could because breathing required some level of brain function.

Even though his lips never left hers, Andi groaned low in her throat when he moved his body away from hers. In a fluid motion, David's hands slid over her hips to the back of her thighs and he lifted her the few inches needed to set her bottom on the table, his hands branding her bare skin when the hem of her dress shifted beneath his touch. With a gentle, but insistent, jerk he brought her body flush against him so she balanced near the edge and his denim-clad hips pushed between her thighs. Andi gasped, her head tipping back as reality flashed like a neon sign in her head.

Wake up! This is a dream! This is not going to happen!

David's tongue dipped into her mouth as he tipped her back slightly. Everything tingled, and her ankles hooked behind his legs before any intelligent and sensible brainwave could find a functioning synapse long enough to warn her she was losing control. Her body hummed with vibrations, and as his mouth shifted its attention from her lips to her throat...he stopped.

Vibration shifted through her again, and through the pounding in her ears, she heard him whisper hoarsely, "Do you need to get that?"

Andi blinked and slowly uncurled her fingers from his shirt, leaning back to look at his face. Every inch of her skin was flushed, and even the simple sundress felt restrictive and smothering, especially when his large hand rested on her thigh, and the pad of his thumb brushed the inside of her knee. It took everything she had to focus on his face to realize he'd asked her a question. His eyes were dark, his irises large and intense, and his rapid breath warmed her already-fevered cheeks.

Vibration again...Andi blinked again...*Work, brain! Work!*

"Your phone...do you need to answer it?"

Reality clicked back into place, and Andi looked slightly behind her to the small folded phone on the table now bounced and slid on the Formica as it vibrated again. David's hand left her thigh—the spot suddenly feeling cold and abandoned—and picked it up, holding it up so she could see the screen.

MAGS

"Do you need to answer it?" he asked again.

Andi shook her head. "No."

He set the phone down, but by then she had been given the two whole seconds needed for her brain to work again, her heart to slow just a few beats so it wasn't going to break free of her chest, and her breathing to catch up with the severe lack of oxygen in her lungs. She watched him set the phone down as if that single action were the most important thing in the world and clenched her hands in her lap. David shifted his weight so he could rest his hands on the edge of the table on either side of her legs and lean down so their faces were level.

"Andi—"

Before he could complete whatever he wanted to say, someone rapped on the trailer door and Andi jumped with a short yelp. David's hands slid to her hips as she hopped off the table, steadying her. Which was good since her knees seemed to no longer have functioning ligaments.

"Yeah?" she called out, her voice croaking. She cleared her throat and tried again. "Yeah?"

"It's April, I'm looking for David. Benton needs him. Do you know where he is?"

"I'm in here," David answered, and Andi shot him a shocked look.

Why not tell the whole crew we were just making out like hormonal teenagers, whydontcha?

He grinned, almost as if he knew the reality of her horror. "I'll be right there."

"'Kay," April called back, her voice already distant as she walked away from the trailer.

"Y-you should go," Andi stuttered out, the heat of embarrassment quickly smothering the heat of arousal. Her cheeks burned hot, and she had the almost uncontrollable desire to cross her arms over her body and scurry into the far corner of the table banquette.

"Yeah." He touched her cheek, stroking her skin before nudging her chin up so she had to look at him or close her eyes in denial. Since she couldn't stand there all day with her eyes closed, Andi met his gaze. And the smile on his face made her breath catch all over again. "Probably not the best place for this, huh?"

"Ya think?" she said with a wry chuckle.

He curled a bit of hair behind her ear, the smile never leaving his face. "I believe you, by the way." Andi frowned and his grin widened as he shook his head. "You can't act."

Before she could come back with some buffering, sarcastic one-shot, he kissed her again. Simply this time—just a pressing of their lips together but he hummed softly and the contact ricocheted through her. His hand slid down her spine to rest on the curve of her backside and Andi couldn't breathe.

"I'm glad," he said against her mouth.

He stepped back, and the air around her was suddenly cold and gooseflesh popped up on her bare arms. Andi wanted to say something—*anything*—but nothing would form enough in her head to make it to her throat.

He made it as far as the door, stopping when his fingers curled around the handle. David looked back at her, his eyes skimming from her face to her sandals and back, and Andi held her breath. With a small sound in the back of his throat, he tilted his head to the side with a small jerk and pivoted back to her. "Not yet," he mumbled before coming back to her.

He raised his hands and enveloped her face as he reached her, and Andi only had a split second to take a breath before his open mouth covered hers. Energy and electricity rolled through her, curling in her stomach and she moaned against his mouth. She gasped when he pulled his lips free of hers, only to plant a trail of forceful, almost rough kisses down the side of her throat to her shoulder. He pressed his face into the hollow where her neck and shoulder met, his teeth gently abrading her skin, his fingers pulling aside her dress collar to expose more skin.

Andi whispered his name, not even realizing she wanted to until it passed her lips. One arm tightened around her, pulling her hard against him. Then he let her go, yanked the door open with a hard jerk, and bounded out of the trailer. The small structure shook in the wake of his departure.

Or, maybe that was just Andi's legs finally giving out. She slouched against the edge of the table and pressed a trembling hand against her hot forehead.

The phone vibrated again, and Andi looked down to see Maggie's name on the screen. *That* conversation would have to wait.

Besides, what would she say?

Sorry I didn't answer, Mags. You see...David Bishop...yeah, that's right David Bishop...yep, the guy voted Number Seven on the Hollywood Top Ten Hottest Men of the Year last year...yeah, him. Well, I'm pretty sure we were about to either have sex or something similar right here on my little trailer table. Yep, you heard me right. No, I wasn't asleep. At least, I don't think I was asleep. Stop laughing, Mags, I mean it.

Andi sighed and covered her face with her hands. *Holy Crap!*